To Jennings, Jackson, Jenson and the young at heart!
—The Texas Tenors

To my Ma and Pa, Brigid and Des Fitzgerald
—B.F.

Text copyright (c) 2015 by Harriet Ziefert
Illustrations copyright (c) 2015 by Brian Fitzgerald
"Ruckus on the Ranch" music copyright (c) 2015 by The Texas Tenors

All rights reserved/
CIP data is available.
Published in the United States by
🍎 Blue Apple Books
515 Valley Street
Maplewood, NJ 07040
www.blueapplebooks.com
First edition 06/15
Printed in China
ISBN: 978-1-60905-534-9

10 9 8 7 6 5 4 3 2 1

THE TEXAS TENORS

RUCKUS ON THE RANCH!

ILLUSTRATIONS BY

BRIAN FITZGERALD

BLUE APPLE

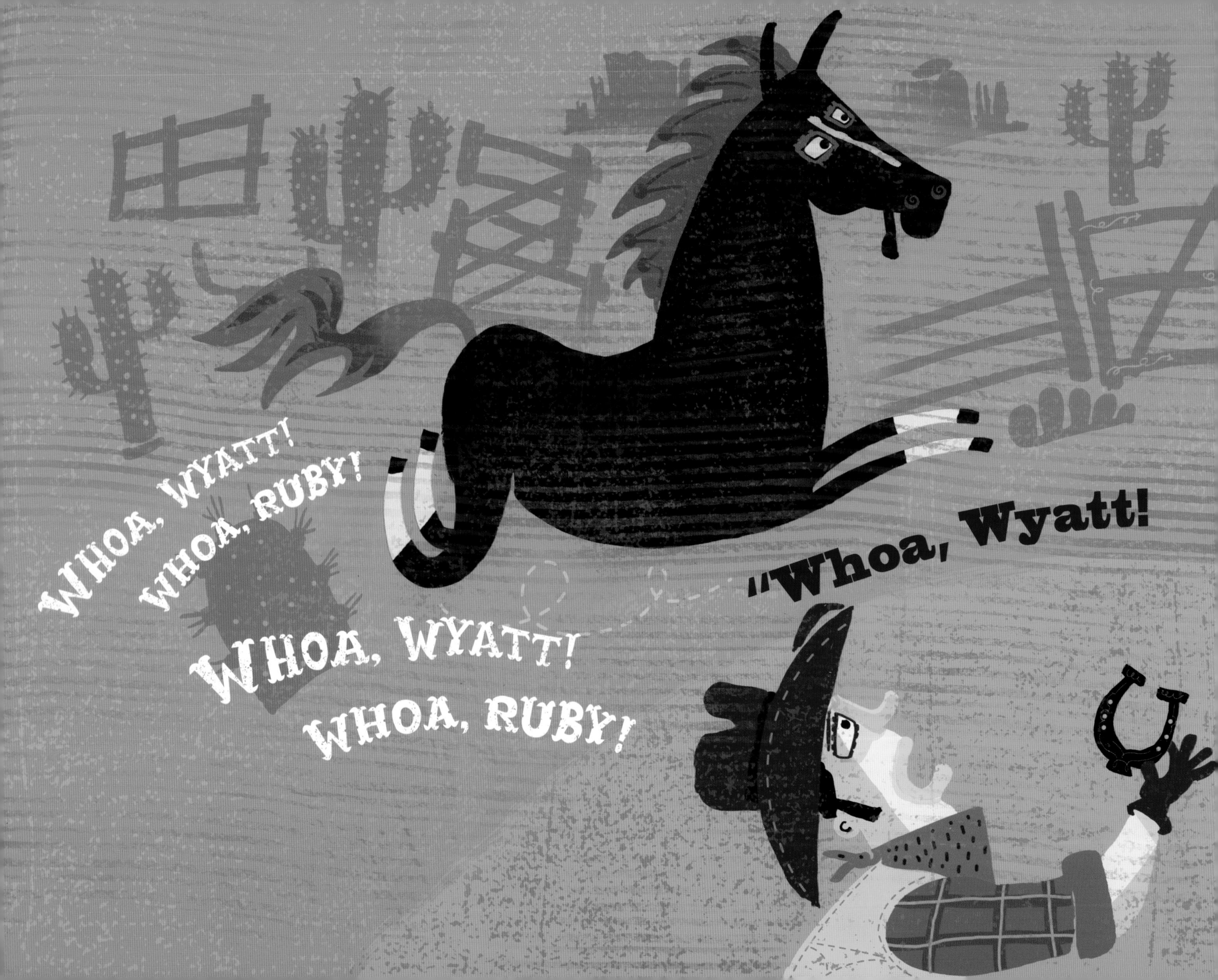

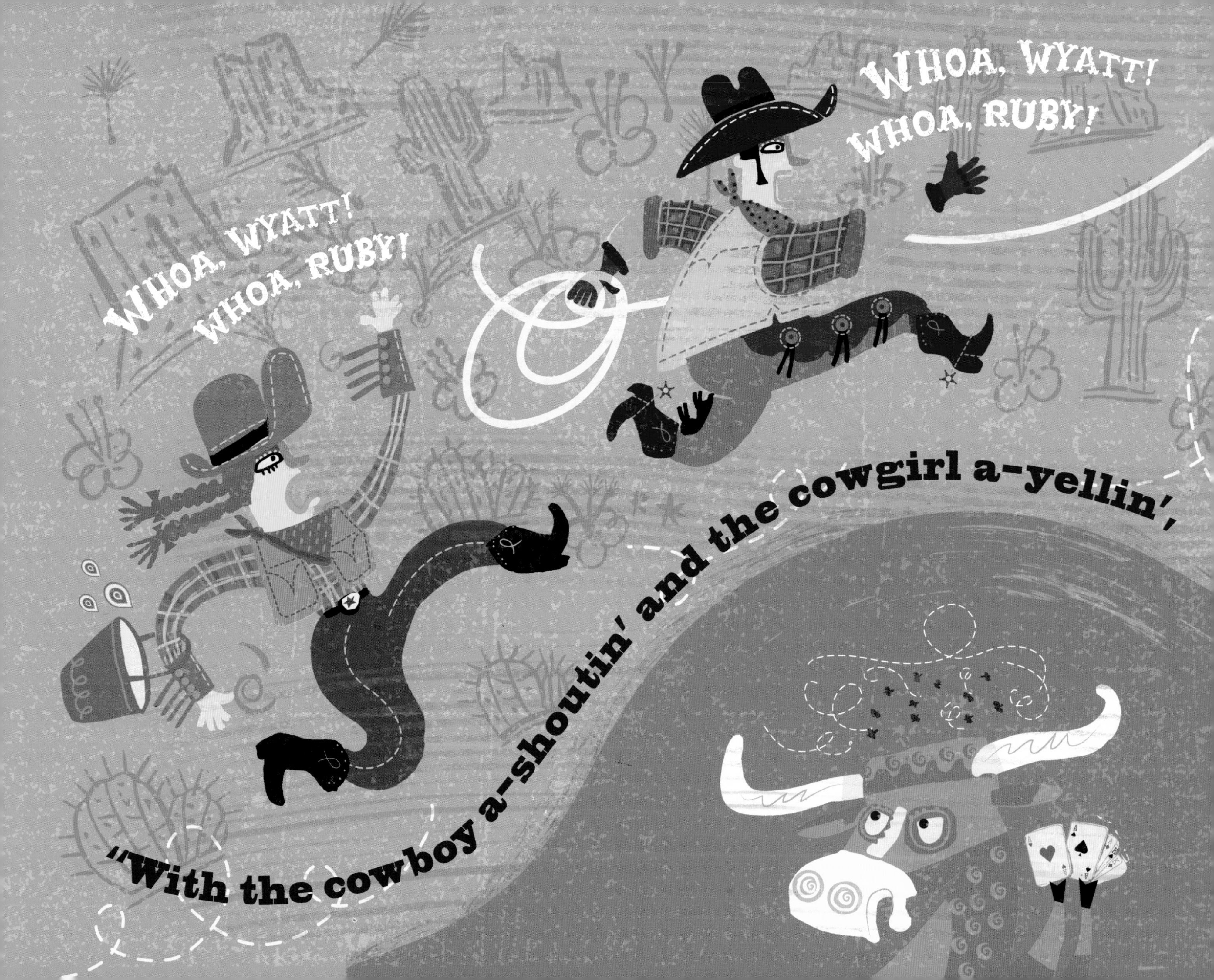

"With the cowboy a-shoutin' and the cowgirl a-yellin',

Y'all get back in place!"   And the longhorn joins the chase!

Y'all get back in place!" And the hog joins the chase!

The chickens hear,

"Whoa, Wyatt!
Whoa, Ruby!
Y'all get back in place!"

CLUCK! CLUCK! CLUCK!

Then the chickens join the chase!

Now the cowboy's **RUNNIN'**,
The cowgirl, too!
The horses gallopin'— **"HEY! HEY!"**

The longhorn's **SNORTIN'**,
The dog goes **a-BARKIN'**,
The hog is **GRUNTIN'**,
The chickens are **a-CLUCKIN'**,
Gettin' in their way—

The hog
plops down.

The horses stand
on the hill.

The cattle sit.

The cowboy snores.
And so does the dog.

The chickens
are very still.

The cowgirl
reads her book.

Oh, what a peaceful ranch! Shhhhh! UNTIL . . .

BUZZZZZZZZZ

Wyatt gets
stung by
a bumblebee!

Oh, no! Here we go again . . .

WHOA, WYATT!

WHOA, RUBY!

Y'all get back in place!

You're causin' a ruckus on the ranch!

You're causin' a ruckus on the ranch!

With the cowboy shoutin',

And the cowgirl a-yellin',

You're causin' a ruckus on the ranch!

One more time now, c'mon!

WHOA, WYATT!

WHOA, RUBY!

Y'all get back in place!

You're causin' a ruckus on the ranch!

You're causin' a ruckus on the ranch!

With the cowboy shoutin',

And the cowgirl a-yellin',

You're causin' a ruckus on the ranch!

YEE-HAW!